Greedy Anansi and his Three Cunning Plans

Stories from West Africa

Contents

Why Anansi the Spider has Eight Long, Thin Legs 2

Anansi, Turtle and the Feast of Yams 10

Anansi, Firefly and Tiger 20

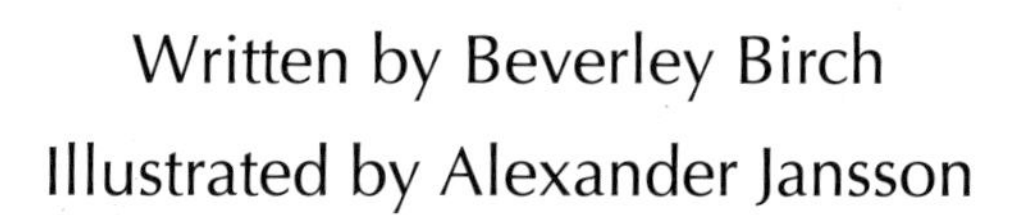

Written by Beverley Birch
Illustrated by Alexander Jansson

Why Anansi the Spider has Eight Long, Thin Legs

There was a time when Anansi's legs were not thin and long, the way they are now. They were very thick and very short and stubby.

This is the story of how they came to change.

Anansi had short legs, but a large belly, and he loved to fill it with good food. Best of all he liked the tasty food cooked by all his friends in the village.

On this particular day, Anansi went to visit Rabbit. Now Rabbit was cooking fresh, ripe greens. At the thought of the wonderful flavour, Anansi's mouth watered and his stomach gurgled.

"Ah!" he cried. "Delicious greens, I see, Rabbit!"

"My dear friend, come and join me for dinner!" said Rabbit. "It's not quite cooked yet, but it'll be ready soon."

But Anansi was not only greedy, he was also lazy. He thought, "If I stay while the greens cook, surely Rabbit will ask for help and give me all kinds of jobs!"

Quick as a flash, Anansi answered, "Oh, Rabbit, that's very kind of you. Of course I will! I have some little tasks to do and I'll be right back. I'll spin a length of web and tie it round my leg. Then we can tie the other end round your cooking pot. When the meal is ready, pull on my web and I'll rush back."

"Good idea!" said Rabbit. So one end of Anansi's web was looped round the pot, and off Anansi went.

He passed Monkey's house, and there – what luck – a delicious aroma wafted out of the door to Anansi's nose.

"Ah! Monkey," he called. "I smell such delicious beans and honey cooking!"

"Well then, my friend, wait until they're cooked, and share them with me," Monkey replied generously.

But Anansi, of course, feared that Monkey would ask for help.

Hurriedly he answered, "Monkey, dear friend, that's kind of you! I'd love to share your meal, but first, I must see to a few things. So here's what we can do. I'll spin a length of web and knot one end round my leg, the other round your cooking pot. When the beans and honey are ready, just pull on my web, and I'll rush back."

"How clever!" said Monkey, so one end of Anansi's web was looped round the pot and away the little spider went.

Anansi walked on.
Such tantalising cooking smells floated around the village!
And there were lots more friends to visit: Tortoise, Hare, Squirrel, Mouse, Fox …

And delight of delights, every one of them was busy making their evening meal.

It's no surprise that for one friend after another he looped a length of web round his leg and the other end round their cooking pot.

Before long, each of Anansi's short stubby legs was attached to the different cooking pots in each friend's home.

Of course, Anansi could only think of the mouth-watering aroma of food that floated around the village, and the scrumptious meals he'd soon be eating.

"I'm really extra clever," Anansi told himself with satisfaction. "I'll have lovely food to eat and not a single job to do in return." He was day-dreaming happily about dishes of sweet potato and honey, and whose meal he'd taste first, when he felt a sudden tug on the web fastened to one leg.

"That's Rabbit calling me to eat his dish of greens!" In a great hurry, Anansi set off towards Rabbit's house.

But there was another tug, on another leg. "Oh, oh! Monkey's calling me to eat his beans and honey."

A third tug, on a third leg! And another! Then another and another … each of Anansi's eight legs was pulled towards a different friend's house!

In a great panic, Anansi threw himself into the river. In the water he struggled to wash away the webs until his legs were free and he could climb out and recover from the fright.

It wasn't long, though, before he saw that his legs were not short and thick and stubby any more. Instead he had eight, long, skinny legs, each stretched and stretched and stretched by the pulling of the webs.

"So that's all I have to show for my clever plan!" he snorted. "Eight spindly legs and eight missed dinners! If I want to eat anything at all today, I'll have to cook it for myself after all!"

Anansi, Turtle and the Feast of Yams

Anansi had fine, ripe yams growing in his garden, just ready for eating. What a meal he'd make from them! Eagerly he dug them up and set them to bake in the oven. How delicious they smelt when they were ready! With glee he sat down to eat.

Just then Turtle knocked at his door.

"Good evening, Anansi," he said wearily. "I've been walking and walking all day! I'm worn out. I smell the tastiest yams baking in your kitchen. Will you share them with a very hungry traveller?"

Now it was the custom in Anansi's country to welcome travellers and give them food. But of course Anansi was very greedy. So it is no surprise that his only thought was, "If I share my yams with Turtle, there won't be so many for me!"

Craftily, he greeted his visitor. "Come in, come in, Turtle. Sit, sit and I'll share my meal."

But just as Turtle helped himself to a yam, Anansi cried, "Oh, Turtle, what dirty hands! You can't eat with such hands!"

Of course it was true, for Turtle's hands were smeared with soil from crawling all day. When he had arrived at Anansi's kitchen he had not yet had a chance to wash.

So he left the table and went to the river. When he'd washed his hands and slowly walked back to Anansi's house, because of course he was more tired than ever now, Anansi was already munching on the yams.

"I wanted to taste them before they got cold," Anansi announced. "Do join me now, Turtle."

But just as Turtle helped himself to a yam, Anansi shouted, "Turtle, what filthy hands! You can't eat with such hands!"

And of course it was true. Turtle's hands were dirty again from crawling back from the river. Again, he washed them, hungrier and more tired than ever. And this time, he came back on the grass all the way, so that his hands would not touch bare soil.

But when he reached the table, Anansi had finished the very last piece of the very last yam. Not even the smallest taste was left for poor, tired, hungry Turtle.

Turtle stayed very calm. "Anansi," he said, "I thank you for sharing your meal with me. Do visit me one day, and I will share mine with you." Then he left Anansi's kitchen and wearily travelled on.

Of course, Anansi kept thinking of that invitation from Turtle. A free meal. He must visit Turtle at once.

He discovered Turtle basking in the sun on a riverbank.

"Ah, Anansi," Turtle greeted him. "I see you've come for supper!" And he plunged down into the river to his house to lay the table.

Soon he rose up to the surface again and invited Anansi to swim down. Then he dived back and began his meal.

Eagerly, Anansi leapt into the water. But he just couldn't follow Turtle. He tried duck-dives, running jumps and belly flops, but nothing worked. However hard he tried to swim to the river bottom, he just bobbed to the surface again. He was frantic, for there was Turtle underwater, calmly eating all the food, and Anansi could do nothing about it.

"I'm too light, that's why," he decided, and quickly loaded stones into his jacket pockets. His plan worked – he was so heavy now that he plummeted straight down through the water to the riverbed and could sit with Turtle at the table.

Such a delicious spread of food greeted him!

He was about to load his plate when Turtle said quietly, "In my country, it's not polite to keep your jacket on at the table."

Eager not to delay the meal any longer, Anansi threw off his jacket …

… and instantly shot right out of the water on to the riverbank.

Worse still, when he pushed his head underwater to look, to his utter fury, Turtle was still calmly enjoying that feast of splendid food, without him.

Anansi, Firefly and Tiger

Firefly kindly invited Anansi the Spider to go egg-hunting with him.

This was exciting – Anansi loved to eat eggs. He rushed to Firefly's house, as arranged, late in the evening, when it was dark enough for Firefly's light to shine.

Together they went out into the fields with their sacks. Firefly opened his wings to shine his light about and make the eggs hidden in the grass gleam a little.

But it was always Anansi who yelled, "I saw it first," and grabbed the egg and pushed it into his sack.

And so it went on. Every egg that Firefly found, Anansi took for himself. Not one was left for Firefly, yet Anansi's sack was full to the top and very heavy. Finally, Firefly had simply had enough, and he spread his wings and flew away home.

Anansi was suddenly quite alone.

Of course, Anansi had not taken the trouble to watch where he was going. He'd left all that worry to Firefly. He had not the slightest idea of the way home. Worse still, he couldn't see at all in the dark, and it was a very black, moonless night.

He stumbled blindly along. He didn't even know if he was travelling further and further from home.

At last he came to a house. But he didn't know whose house it was, or if it was safe, or if the owner would welcome him.

Feeling desperate, Anansi finally found the courage to call out, "Hello!"

"Who's that?" came a deep, rumbly, scary voice.

"Anansi!" replied the little spider.

But it was Tiger whose huge head peered out of the door. Anansi felt very small and very scared.

Anansi, of course, had tricked Tiger many, many times before. But Tiger just said, "Come in, Anansi," and Tiger's wife filled a big pot with water and put it on the fire to boil the eggs from Anansi's sack.

Then Tiger, his wife, and all their children sat down to eat them.

"Have some eggs," Tiger growled at Anansi.

Anansi did not dare. He stayed well away from the hungry tiger family.

When all the eggs were finished, and Anansi wasn't looking, Tiger lowered a lobster into the pot and put eggshells on top. Now it looked as if there were lots of eggs left.

He put the pot where Anansi could reach it. "Stay for the night, Anansi," he said, but his grin showed all his fierce great teeth and Anansi was terrified.

But he was not terrified enough to ignore his hungry belly. When everyone was snoring, Anansi crept to the pot and put his hand inside, at which the lobster pinched him with a claw. Anansi was so shocked he let out a yell.

"Anansi," Tiger enquired from his bed, "is something wrong?"

"I was just bitten by a dog-flea. I'm sorry, Tiger!"

When everyone had settled back to sleep, Anansi tried again to reach an egg. He got another hard pinch from an angry lobster, and he let out another yell.

"Is there really nothing wrong, Anansi?" grumbled Tiger, glaring at him.

"Oh, oh, these dog-fleas are eating me," Anansi protested.

Tiger growled. Then he snarled. Then he roared, "Dog-fleas? Dog-fleas! In my house! You say this, when we have fed you and given you a warm, safe place to sleep!" And he leapt out of bed towards Anansi.

Anansi raced for the door
and shot out of sight.

Tiger stopped. He licked his
lips and grinned again as
he watched the little spider
running and running for his life.

Of course, Anansi never returned to Tiger's house. And surprise, surprise, every time he went to see Firefly, Firefly's wife said sweetly, "Oh dear, Anansi, my husband is away again. But of course you must call by again next month."

Anansi never again found that field where Firefly had taken him – the one where all the eggs were hidden. And it didn't take him long to see that his greed, in the end, had given him absolutely nothing.

Anansi's plans

Anansi wanted to get food from his friends without doing any work to help them.

Anansi didn't want to share any of his food with Turtle, but wanted to eat Turtle's food later.

Anansi didn't want to share any eggs with Firefly.

Ideas for reading

Written by Clare Dowdall PhD
Lecturer and Primary Literacy Consultant

Learning objectives: infer characters' feelings in fiction; use syntax, context and word structure to build a store of vocabulary; empathise with characters and debate moral dilemmas portrayed in texts; use beginning, middle and end to write narratives in which events are sequenced logically and conflicts resolved

Curriculum links: Citizenship: Choices

Interest words: cunning, yams, stomach, aroma, generously, hurriedly, scrumptious, tastiest, custom, craftily, frantic, plummeted

Resources: whiteboard, ICT

Getting started

This book can be read over two or more reading sessions.

- Look at the front cover together. Ask children whether they know any Anansi stories, and to recall any that they have heard before.
- Based on the cover, discuss what children think Anansi's character might be like and what kind of stories might be contained within the book, e.g. stories with morals; stories about what happens if you are greedy.
- Discuss the word *cunning*. Check that children know what it means, and explain it is an adjective or describing word. Read the contents page and challenge children to locate all the words that are describing words: *greedy, three, cunning, eight, long, thin.* Note these words on the whiteboard for later.

Reading and responding

- Read pp2–3 aloud with the children. Ask them to suggest what they think will happen next in the story. Encourage children to reread pp2–3 to enrich their predictions based on reading.
- Ask children to read pp4–5. Discuss the information provided about the character of Anansi so far, and identify words that describe him. Support children to make inferences by suggesting their own words to describe Anansi. Add these words to the list started earlier.